Sleepy Farm

written by Rob and Ouvrielle Holmes

illustrated by Michael Terry

Deep in the country lies a farm,
   where the sun and stars cast a magic charm.
The animals have lots of fun,
   well all, that is, apart from one!

Charlie Chicken had a busy day,
he made a house from a bale of hay.

Millie Moo Cow learned to dance,
  you should have seen her twirl and prance!

Desmond Duck designed a boat,
he said it really helped him float!

And Holly Horse played with her kite,
    it really was an awesome sight!

But Percy Pig just lay there snoring,
no wonder they called him 'Mr Boring'!

So why did Percy sleep all day,
    instead of playing in the hay?
Why was he always in a mood?
    Why was he cross? Why was he rude?

The sun then set behind the hill,
and in a wink...

Turn your Gro-clock to 'night-time' mode now.

...the farm went still.

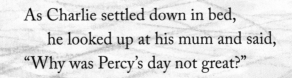

As Charlie settled down in bed,
  he looked up at his mum and said,
"Why was Percy's day not great?"

"Because he's into bed too late!"

Millie rested on the floor,
  and nestled in her comfy straw,
  "Dad, why does Percy have no fun?"

"Because he's up before the sun!"

Desmond snuggled down to rest,
warm and cosy in his nest.
He asked his mum, "Why's Percy lazy?"

"He's tired and drives his parents crazy!"

Then Holly had a bright idea,
and drew the others round to hear.
They saved some money in a sock...

...and bought the pig a special clock!

Now Percy sleeps from dusk 'til dawn,
and plays all day without a yawn.
He frolics with his new-found friends,
and falls asleep as daytime ends.

And through the night, the stars shine down,
keeping watch on field and town.
The animals dream of games to play,
as stars begin to fade away.